A Mermaid's Tale

Meet a host of underwater creatures
on an adventure into
the deep blue sea

Dominic Guard

First edition for the United States
and Canada published in 2007 by
Barron's Educational Series, Inc.
©2006 Andromeda Children's Books
An imprint of Pinwheel Ltd
Created and produced by
Andromeda Children's Books,
an imprint of Pinwheel Ltd
Winchester House, 259–269 Old Marylebone Road,
London, NW1 5XJ, UK

Author: Dominic Guard
Illustrator: Maria Woods
Art Director: Miranda Kennedy
Designer: Patricia Hopkins
Editorial Manager: Isabel Thomas
Production Director: Clive Sparling

ISBN-13: 978-0-7641-9307-1
ISBN-10: 0-7641-9307-4
Library of Congress Control No.
2006938825

Printed in China

9 8 7 6 5 4 3 2 1

BARRON'S

Contents

Beatrice and the Mermaid

Once upon a time, a long time ago, a young girl named Beatrice sat upon a beach. She had been told by her father to sit still and amuse herself while he fished all day. Her father stood very still at the edge of the ocean.

Bea (that is what her friends called her) looked at the horizon longingly, though she didn't quite know what it was that she longed for.

She walked along the beach a little, sat beside a rock pool, and stared into it. She watched as the crabs scuttled quickly away and the shrimps hid from her.

"Don't be scared of me," Bea whispered to the creatures in the pool.

At that moment a sparkling silver fish flipped out of the pool and flapped about beside Bea.

As it struggled for life, Bea gently scooped it up in her hands and put it back into the pool. When the fish touched the water the most amazing thing happened: it turned into a beautiful, tiny young mermaid.

The mermaid swam around the pool and, as she swam, she grew and grew. By the time she leaped out of the pool to sit beside Bea, they were the same size! They looked at each other in amazement before the mermaid announced: "My name is Melia, daughter of Neptune. A jealous Siren cast a spell to make sure I would remain a fish until a human saved my life. I have waited a long time to find one as gentle as you."

"It's true some humans are unkind to fish—and, for that matter, to other people." agreed Bea.

"To thank you I should like to take you to meet my father, Neptune, and to show you the magic of the deep blue sea."

"I can't go anywhere," said Bea tearfully. "My father told me to sit here."

Melia smiled a knowing smile and gave Bea a brightly colored shell to wear around her neck. She said, "With this shell, time will stand still while we travel. With this shell, you will be able to breathe beneath the waves."

Bea held the shell to her ear and heard beautiful mermaid music. On the beach, time had frozen. The lighthouse had stopped blinking, and Bea's father stood as still as a statue. Bea placed the shell around her neck and slowly lowered her head into the rock pool. She could see and breathe under the water!

A shrimp tickled Bea under the chin and a crab playfully pinched her nose. She wanted to stare into the pool forever. But Melia announced that it was time for their adventure to begin.

Hand in hand, Bea walked and Melia flopped along to the shore. Bea slipped off her shoes and left them neatly together by the water's edge.

With the magic shell held tightly in her hand, Bea looked to the end of the beach where her father stood, as if frozen. "I promise he will not notice you have gone," Melia assured her.

The new friends plunged into the cool water. Bea held Melia's hand tightly as they swam along the surface.

A dolphin swam beside them and called out:

"Welcome back, Melia! You've been away too long!"

"Thank you, Prince of the Sea!" Melia called back.

Bea joined in too:

"Thank you, Prince of the Sea! Thank you! Thank you, Melia!" she called out.

The adventure had begun...

Creatures of Land and Sea

Bea and Melia swam on either side of the dolphin, all three soaring through the air and diving into the surf. The dolphin soon spotted some of his friends and went off to play with them. But other creatures that love both the air and the water quickly joined the friends.

Seals, otters, and penguins now leaped and played beside them. They all joined in a competition to see how long they could stay under the water. Melia and a very surprised Bea always won. "It's funny because I don't do very well in my swimming lessons," said Bea.

"You must have very good swimmers in your class," giggled an otter.

"Do you ever stop laughing?" asked Bea.

"Only when they go too deep," interrupted Melia.

"Many years ago my father, Neptune, granted them the gift of the big breath. They used to need magic shells to swim as you do now, but not anymore. However, they stay in the shallows and cannot reach the deep blue where we are going."

"Yes, that's true, but I can walk on two legs like a human!" chirped a penguin. "And I can swim faster than the fastest wave," barked a seal.

The seals, otters, and penguins continued beside them until Melia decided that their adventure must continue. She said: "Goodbye, fellow creatures! We must leave you now and go to the deep blue!" With that, Melia clasped Bea's hand, and together they swam toward the deep water that seals, otters, and penguins could not reach.

Danger in the Depths

M elia swam deeper and deeper, guiding Bea into the depths of the ocean. Bea heard humming and ringing in her ears and her heart beat like a big bass drum. She clasped Melia's hand as tightly as she could. The ocean became cooler around them.

Bea looked up to the sky and could still see the seals and penguins swishing across the water's surface. She wished she were still with them. She was not used to breathing under water, let alone deep, deep water, so she held onto her shell as tightly as she could.

Melia clasped Bea's hand tightly as well and said: "You are right to be nervous, for not everything in the ocean is friendly."

"That's all right," replied Bea bravely, "not everyone on land is friendly either."

"You must be alert at all times," continued Melia.

"What's a 'Lert'?" asked Bea.

"Alert is not a thing," laughed Melia. "Being alert means we must watch out at all times for...shhhh," and the mermaid whispered, "...sharks!"

"What do we do if we see a shark?" shivered Bea.

"Stay close to me. Sharks are very fast, but they have no brakes; they are hopeless at stopping."

Around Bea the ocean felt colder than ice and she wondered if this adventure was a good idea. "How does that help us?" she asked.

"Just make sure we have a hard rock behind us," whispered Melia. "Anyway, my little fish friends usually group together to make the shape of a monster fish to scare the sharks away."

"Where are your little fish friends?" asked Bea, but Melia swam on without answering. The ocean felt colder still, and looked darker too. There were no signs of small fish as the two little swimmers swam further and deeper.

The Song of the Sirens

Bea noticed that her ears had stopped ringing, and she felt as though she was becoming used to breathing under water. Suddenly she heard the most magical music. "I love this music!" Bea called out excitedly.

Melia looked alarmed and swam on quickly.

"My friend, you can hear the Sirens. They are trying to lure you into danger. You must ignore them! Not everything that sounds good is good."

"Do you mean like ice cream? That always sounds good, but isn't really good for you," Bea asked.

"Yes, that's it!" Melia laughed. "I must find my mirror. It's the only way to scare those jealous, ugly, fish-people away. I lost it when the Siren cast the spell upon me." The friends were interrupted by a voice from a dark cave:

"Welcome Melia, come in, come in! I've waited so long to tell you: I have your comb and mirror! I buried them safely here when the Siren turned you into a fish!"

Bea realized that the voice came from a little crab. He dug into the sand until he found Melia's lost treasures. The mermaid somersaulted with joy at the sight of her favorite things. Bea realized that they must be very special indeed.

Melia began combing her long hair and gazing into her mirror. Soon Bea became bored and asked, "Are we at the bottom of the ocean?"

"Oh no," said the helpful crab, "We are only on the continental shelf."

"We've come all this way down and we're only on a shelf?" exclaimed Bea.

Melia thanked the crab, and fastened her mirror and comb to the shell belt around her waist. She took hold of Bea's hand, and they swam on.

Exploring the Coral Jungle

T he friends swam on in silence. Soon Bea
noticed that they were no longer swimming
downward. The ocean was becoming warmer
again. Without warning, they arrived at the edge
of a multicolored jungle under the ocean.

Bea stared in amazement at the magical forest.
Hundreds of brightly-colored fish appeared all
around them and waved their fins at Melia, who
began to comb her hair once more.

"Now I can look my best again! I thought we
should meet some more of my friends before we
continue toward the deep! These
are my favorite little fish, my
pretty coral reef friends!"

Bea gasped with delight at
the brightly painted parrot
fish, butterfly fish, starfish,
and bright blue damsel fish that

lit up the water around her. But she did not really understand how combing your hair underwater could make you look your best.

Then Bea realized that Melia had let go of her hand for the first time. She was swimming alone, without holding onto her mermaid friend. The pair played hide and seek with the fish of the coral reef. Every time Melia found a fish, it would ask if it were the most beautiful of all, and Melia would answer: "Yes. Apart from me, you are the most beautiful."

"It is strange that the fish ask if they are the most beautiful when they are all so beautiful," Bea remarked.

"It is no stranger than humans thinking money is better than seashells!" replied Melia.

"That's true!" laughed Bea. "Now it is my turn to hide!"

"Yes, beautiful Bea, it is your turn to hide and be found!" laughed Melia.

Creatures of the Reef

Bea loved swimming alone. She was just thinking how busy everyone seemed when a huge leathery turtle floated by and asked, "Would you like a lift, young lady?"

Bea climbed onto the turtle's back and they slowly toured the coral reef. The turtle asked Bea where she was going and Bea replied that she was going to the deep with Melia.

"Take care, for the deep is dangerous," warned the wise old turtle.

But Bea did not want to hear of danger. She swam off to explore a cave. A moment later she swam straight back out, screaming, "Aaaaah! There's a..."

"... very grumpy old eel in there!" smiled the turtle.

"How did you know?" asked Bea.

"When you are two hundred years old, you know these things," answered the turtle.

The wise turtle took Bea to watch the hermit crabs scuttling to and fro across the sand. "These little fellows have no shells of their own," he explained. "So they use other animals' old shells, and ask sponges and sea urchins to decorate them so that dangerous creatures cannot see them."

"Why do sponges and sea urchins do that?" Bea was curious to know.

"Because the hermit crabs share all their meals with them, so everyone is very happy with the arrangement," replied the turtle.

Melia called out to Bea that it was time to leave. As Bea swam to Melia, she called out, "I am very happy with our arrangement!"

The turtle smiled as he waved goodbye to the two little swimmers.

Down into the Deep Blue

Melia once more held her friend's hand and explained that now it was time to go where no human has gone before, where there is no time, or tide, or weather. Once more they swam down, down, down, and deeper still. Once more the ocean became cold, and then much, much darker, as if night was falling.

"If there is no time down here, why is night falling?" asked Bea.

"Night is not falling, it is we who are falling. Sometimes you must fall or you will never be able to pick yourself up," laughed Melia, as it became darker still.

Then Melia plucked her mirror from her belt. It began to shine and guided them through the inky blackness. As they followed the bright glow of the mirror, they were suddenly blinded by the glare of other bright lights. These were the glares and stares of deep-sea  fish that make their own light. Lantern fish and angler fish called out with glee as their glaring lights shone upon Melia's magical mirror.

"So good to see your glow with our glare," they said. "Are you going home at last?"

"I am going home once more!" said Melia. She flicked her tail with joy, then checked her reflection in her mirror. Once more, Bea was blinded by the glare of the deep-sea fish. She felt alone and frightened in the dark, especially when the fish asked Melia whether her father would be angry to see a human so deep.

"This human saved my mermaid life," explained Melia to the deep-sea fish. "She is not just any human." Then Melia turned to Bea and told her, "Don't worry! These fish can only see as far as their light shines and no further." But Bea did not feel welcome or safe in this dark, deep place near the bottom of the ocean.

The Gate to the Kingdom

On they swam in the darkness, losing their way every time Melia checked her hair in her mirror. Bea closed her eyes and wished Melia would pay more attention to the deep, dark journey. Bea had no intention of letting go of Melia's hand or her shell.

Darkness followed velvety darkness. Finally Bea felt a glimmer of light upon her eyelids. She opened her eyes as Melia's grip loosened.

She had never awoken to such beauty. In front of them stood the gates to Neptune's kingdom. The bottom of the ocean was lighter than a new dawn!

But now the gate moved! It was not a solid gate as we know them on land. It moved, it changed color, and shape. Bea realized that it was actually a magical giant squid.

And now the squid spoke in a booming voice:

"Welcome home Melia! Now you know what it is like to change your shape, to be a fish. Now you understand what it is like to be a magical squid!"

"Yes, I do, but I'm so pleased to be a Mermaid and to be home. I never want to change again!"

Bea thought Melia sounded rather royal, now she was home. The squid smiled as if he were the wise turtle. Then he nodded and a procession of sea horses appeared, the most loyal of all sea creatures, to guide Bea and Melia on the last part of their journey.

After the long, dark journey, Bea was overjoyed to find that it was light and warm at the bottom of the ocean. She followed Melia into a chariot pulled by hundreds of sea horses.

A Royal Return

As the chariot was pulled along the ocean floor, hundreds of sea creatures joined the procession, blowing into seashells to make magical music. Everything was more colorful than anything on land, or even in the coral reef.

In the far distance, Melia spotted her father's beard, or at least the very end of it. Slowly they followed this tremendously long beard until they reached great Neptune himself, sitting on a coral throne. Beneath his huge beard it was hard to tell if he was smiling or frowning.

That is, until he spoke, in a huge, and rather angry, voice: "Welcome home, my daughter. I have missed you. But why have you shown a human our deep sea secret?"

"Father of the secrets of the seven seas! I am so pleased to see you too. I have brought Bea because it was her kindness that changed me back into myself and broke the Siren's spell," explained Melia.

Bea bowed and said, "Pleased to meet you," but she could not tell if Neptune was pleased to meet her. He stayed very still, like her own father when he was fishing. Then, he signaled with his trident and all the sea creatures danced with delight at Melia's return. Bea sat feeling very alone. A tear ran down her cheek, though no one knew, because tears are wet and salty, just like seawater. Tears are the sea and the sea is tears, thought Bea.

As Bea sat alone and Melia danced with her friends, Sirens jealously watched the party from an old shipwreck. They were determined to spoil the fun!

A Narrow Escape

S oon Neptune left the party, to plan the tides for the following day. As the dancing slowed, Bea once more heard the Sirens' magical music, but she remembered that not everything that sounds good is good, and quickly tried to find Melia to tell her. Bea could see that Melia did not have her mirror. No wonder she lost it before! Bea quickly found the mirror and swam towards Melia, shouting out, "I can hear the music!"

Not quite understanding, Melia called back, "It's wonderful, isn't it? Come and dance!"

Before Bea could move, Sirens leaped out from the shipwreck, grabbing her ankles with their slimy tentacles, and began to pull her away.

Bea screamed out as loudly as she could:
"Melia, come quickly, as quickly as you can!"

At once Melia answered the call but, as she swam towards Bea, the slimy Sirens grabbed her too. Bea quickly threw the mirror to her friend, and Melia pointed it at the Sirens. They could not stand the sight of themselves and swam away, screaming and screeching sickeningly.

Melia was so relieved that Bea had helped her.

"I knew I could trust you!" she gasped. "I'm sorry I left you alone at the party. Where is my father when I need him?"

"He went to work," said Bea.

"Sometimes I think he cares more for his work than he does for me," sobbed Melia as a fat tear rolled down her face.

Although people cannot usually see tears in the sea, Bea could see it. The two friends both missed their fathers, and they cried and comforted one another.

A Gift from Neptune

As the friends' tears disappeared in the ocean, Melia began to feel very angry with her father, and set off at once to find him. As Melia approached Neptune, he looked up from his ocean charts. Before he could speak, Melia began:

"Father of the seas, you are mighty and magical, but you are not a good father. Your work is more important than I am. You were not there when once more the Sirens came to take me. Bea, who you do not trust, saved me again."

There was a long silence. Eventually Neptune spoke, slowly and gravely: "Bea, you are a true friend to my daughter and therefore to the ocean. I am sure you are a good friend on land too, where many are not friendly."

"Sirens and sharks aren't friendly either," Bea pointed out.

"You are wise, too," smiled Neptune.

Suddenly, with a flick of his trident, he shone a bright light upon Bea's magic shell. Bea studied the shell closely, but it looked just the same. Melia smiled, then spoke. "Thank you, father of the sea. Now it is time for me to take Bea home."

"Yes, my beloved daughter," said Neptune, "and this time I will dance with joy on your return."

The friends swam up toward the surface, but as journey home began, a dark shadow appeared above them. "Shark!" shouted Bea.

"Be calm," whispered Melia, who pulled Bea in front of a rock and turned to face the terrible fish. The shark sped toward them. Bea closed her eyes tightly, trusting Melia. At the very last moment Melia flicked her tail and dodged out of the way, pulling Bea with her.

The shark's snout crumpled on the rock, and he swam off looking bashful. Bea and Melia giggled and sped toward the surface.

Earth, Air, and Water

As they made their way upward, Bea waved farewell to all her new friends: the lantern and butterfly fish, the ancient turtle, and even the grumpy eel. Eventually they reached the surface and once more breathed in air.

"It tickles when I breathe air," giggled Melia.

"That's funny; it tickled when I breathed water!" laughed Bea.

They swam along the surface, riding the white waves as though they were wild horses. Penguins and flying fish joined them.

"It's amazing," shrieked Bea excitedly, "All around us are fish that fly and birds that swim. And I am a girl who can swim and you are a mermaid who..."

"... doesn't know where she is!" interrupted Melia.

They looked at the beach in front of them, but it did not look at all familiar. Bea wondered if she would ever get home. Then they heard the cackle of the dolphin who had danced with them at the start of their journey.

"Are you lost again, Melia?" he asked.

"Yes, a little bit. Land all looks the same to me," admitted Melia.

Perhaps it would help if you didn't look in your mirror so much," teased Bea.

The dolphin guided them to the beach they had left. It had not changed at all. As they swam ashore, the lighthouse began to blink and Bea's father began to fish again. Bea's shoes had not moved but sand had blown into them. "Now I love the ocean," she said, "but I still hate getting sand in my shoes."

Back to the Beach

Melia and Bea moved up the beach and sat together beside the rock pool. They were exhausted after their adventure. They watched shrimps scurry around the pool as if it were their own tiny ocean. Seagulls squawked in the sky above them. A dog played in the sand.

At last Melia spoke the words that Bea did not want to hear: "Time is moving forward once more, and I must return to my home, where there is not time, or tide, or weather."

"On land you can see tears clearly," sobbed Bea.

"I know," wept Melia and their tears dripped into the rock pool, as if it were raining. Melia flopped down to the water's edge, looked back at her friend once more and said: "Beautiful, kind Bea, this is not goodbye—only farewell, my friend." She vanished as magically as she had appeared.

Bea sat feeling very alone. She missed her friend terribly. She held her shell to her ear to see if she could still hear music. But to her surprise, she heard the seagulls shouting:

"Lovely day today!"

She heard the dog barking on the sand:

"I wish someone would throw me a stick!"

For Neptune had given her the power to understand the creatures of the land as well as those of the ocean!

Bea ran to her father, who was packing up for the day. He was thrilled to see her and did a dance of joy, as if he knew she had been away a long, long time. Bea clutched her magic shell and looked toward the horizon just in time to see Melia's tail disappearing into the ocean waves. But she smiled, as she knew her friend had not gone forever.